THE WINTER ROOM

GARY PAULSEN

SCHOLASTIC INC.

Copyright © 1989 by Gary Paulsen

This book was originally published in hardcover by Orchard Books in 1989.

All rights reserved. Published by Scholastic Inc., *Publishers since 1920*. SCHOLASTIC and associated logos are trademarks and/or registered trademarks of Scholastic Inc.

The publisher does not have any control over and does not assume any responsibility for author or third-party websites or their content.

No part of this publication may be reproduced, stored in a retrieval system, or transmitted in any form or by any means, electronic, mechanical, photocopying, recording, or otherwise, without written permission of the publisher. For information regarding permission, write to Scholastic Inc., Attention: Permissions Department, 557 Broadway, New York, NY 10012.

This book is a work of fiction. Names, characters, places, and incidents are either the product of the author's imagination or are used fictitiously, and any resemblance to actual persons, living or dead, business establishments, events, or locales is entirely coincidental.

ISBN 978-1-338-71393-0

10 9 8 7 6 5 4 3 2 1   21 22 23 24 25

Printed in the U.S.A.   40

This edition first printing 2021

For my father,
with great love

~ TUNING

If books could be more, could show more, could own more, this book would have smells. . . .

It would have the smells of old farms; the sweet smell of new-mown hay as it falls off the oiled sickle blade when the horses pull the mower through the field, and the sour smell of manure steaming in a winter barn. It would have the sticky-slick smell of birth when the calves come and they suck for the first time on the rich, new milk; the dusty smell of winter hay dried and stored in the loft waiting to be dropped down to the cattle; the pungent fermented smell of the chopped corn silage when it is brought into the manger on the silage fork. This book would have the smell of new potatoes sliced and frying in light pepper on a woodstove burning dry pine, the damp smell of leather mittens steaming on the back of the stovetop, and the acrid smell of the slop bucket by the door when the lid is lifted and the potato peelings are dumped in—but it can't.

Books can't have smells.

If books could be more and own more and give more, this book would have sound. . . .

It would have the high, keening sound of the six-foot bucksaws as the men pull them back and forth through the trees to cut pine for paper pulp; the grunting-gassy sounds of the work teams snorting and slapping as they hit the harness to jerk the stumps out of the ground. It would have the chewing sounds of cows in the barn working at their cuds on a long winter's night; the solid thunking sound of the ax coming down to split stovewood, and the piercing scream of the pigs when the knife cuts their throats and they know death is at hand—but it can't.

Books can't have sound.

And finally if books could be more, give more, show more, this book would have light. . . .

Oh, it would have the soft gold light—gold

with bits of hay dust floating in it—that slips through the crack in the barn wall; the light of the Coleman lantern hissing flat-white in the kitchen; the silver-gray light of a middle winter day, the splattered, white-night light of a full moon on snow, the new light of dawn at the eastern edge of the pasture behind the cows coming in to be milked on a summer morning—but it can't.

Books can't have light.

If books could have more, give more, be more, show more, they would still need readers, who bring to them sound and smell and light and all the rest that can't be in books.

The book needs you.

G.P.

SPRING

In the spring everything is soft.

Wayne is my older brother by two years and so he thinks he knows more than I can ever know. He said Miss Halverson, who teaches eighth grade, told him spring was a time of awakening, but I think she's wrong. And Wayne is wrong too.

Or maybe it's just that Miss Halverson wants it to be that way. But she has never seen spring at our farm and if she did, if she would come out and see it, she would know it's not a time of awakening at all. Unless she means awakening of smells.

It's a time for everything to get soft. And melty. And when it all starts to melt and get soft the smells come out. In northern Minnesota where we live, the deep cold of winter keeps things from smelling. When we clean the barn and throw the manure out back it just freezes in a pile. When chickens die or sheep die or even if a cow dies it is left out back on the manure pile because like Uncle David says we're all fertilizer in the end.

Uncle David is old. So old we don't even know for sure how old he is. He says when he dies he wants to be thrown on the manure pile just like the dead animals, but he might be kidding.

The main thing is that no matter what Miss Halverson tells Wayne, in the spring everything gets soft and it's an awful mess. When the dead animals on the pile thaw out they bring early flies and that means maggots and that means stink that stops even my father, or Uncle David, or Nels when they open the back door of the barn to let the cows out.

"Shooosh," Father says when he opens the door of the barn on a spring morning to let the cows out after milking. The smell from the pile makes him sneeze.

Just outside the door the cows sink in until

their bellies are hung up in manure and slop and they have to skid and lunge to get to solid ground.

Sometimes my father and Wayne and I have to get in the muck in back of the barn and heave on the cows to help them through. There's not a part of it that can be called fun. I'm small for eleven, and the goop comes up to my crotch. When I bear down and push on some old cow's leg and she comes loose I almost always fall on my face.

That makes Wayne laugh. He's always ready to laugh when I do something dumb. And when he laughs I get mad and take after him. Then Father has to grab me by the back of my coat and hold me until I cool down—hanging there dripping manure like some old sick cat—and I can't think of any part of it that makes me come up with an awakening.

It's just soft. And stinky.

We live on a farm on the edge of a forest that reaches from our door in Minnesota all the way up to Hudson's Bay. Uncle David says the trees there are stunted and small, the people are short and round, and the polar bears have a taste for human flesh. That's how Uncle David says it when he goes into his stories. He says he's seen such things . . . but that's for later.

The farm has eighty-seven cleared acres. My father says each tree pulled to clear it was like pulling a tooth. I saw him use the team once to take out a popple stump that wasn't too big and he had the veins sticking out on the horses' necks so they looked like ropey cords before that stump let go.

The woods are tight all around the farm, come right down to the edge of it, but the fields are clean and my father says the soil is good, as good as any dirt in the world, and we get corn and oats and barley and flax and some wheat.

There are six of us in the family. My mother and father and my brother Wayne and my uncle David, who isn't really my uncle but sort of my great-uncle who is very old, and Nels, who is old like David.

We all live in a wooden house with white board siding. Downstairs are four rooms. The kitchen, which is big and has a plank table in it and a wood stove with a shiny nickel top, is my favorite. It smells all the time of fresh baked bread because Mother always has rolls rising or cooking or cooling and the smell makes my mouth water.

Next to the kitchen is a room with a table and a piano and four chairs around the table. In all my life and in all of Wayne's life, and as near as we can figure in all my parents' lives, nobody has ever sat at the table or played the old piano. Once a month, when the *Farm Gazette* comes with the pictures of Holsteins or work horses painted on the cover, my mother puts the magazine in the middle of the table in the dining room—that's what she calls it—and the magazine stays there until the next month when the new one comes. Once I asked her why. "For color and decoration," she said.

Only one time did I ever see anybody take the magazine up. Father came in of a morning after chores and picked the magazine off the table and made a comment about the cow on the cover. Mother took it from him, as if he were a kid. She put it back on the table, postioned it just so, the way she always does, and I never saw anybody move the magazine again.

Next to the room with the piano and table— we have never once dined in the room so I don't know why Mother calls it the dining room—is the winter room. Wayne says Miss Halverson showed him a picture of a house in a city and they had a room called a living room, and that's what our winter room is—the living room. But that sounds stupid to me. We live everywhere in the house, except for the room with the table and piano, so why have any one place called the living room?

We call it the winter room because we spend the winter there. In one corner is a wood stove with mica windows so you can see the flame. There are two chairs by the stove, wooden chairs with carved flowers on the back boards. They belong to Uncle David and Nels. Next to each chair is a coffee can for spitting snoose when they chew inside the house. Across from the stove is a large easy chair only a little worn, where Father sits in the winter. Next to the chair is an old horsehide couch with large, soft cushions where Mother sits and Wayne and I sometimes sit, though we usually sit on the floor in front of the stove where the heat can hit our faces and we can see the flames.

Next to the winter room is the downstairs bedroom where Mother and Father sleep on an old iron bed with a feather mattress.

Up a narrow wooden stairway there are two more rooms, built under the angle of the roof. One is for Wayne and me. We have bunk beds on one side and a board shelf on the other where Wayne keeps his baseball glove—he's going to play professional ball when he grows up and leaves the farm—and I have a box of arrowheads I've found. Most of them are small black-stone heads with razor-sharp edges that Uncle David says come from ancient times and were used for hunting birds. But one head is large, a spearhead Uncle David says, made of gray flint. I have that one in a case that used to hold an Elgin turnip pocket watch. Sometimes I take the case out from under my mattress and just look at the spearhead and think what it must have been like to hunt with it, throw it and see it hit a deer or one of the large buffalo they used to have.

The other room upstairs belongs to Uncle David and Nels. It is a little larger than our room and Wayne and I have only been in it a few times. They each have a bed, one on each side of the room back under the slant that comes down with the roof, and a small dresser with a kerosene lamp in the middle so they can blow it out from bed without having to get uncovered.

In the winter there is no heat upstairs and you don't want to get uncovered unless you have to go to the pee bucket in the hall. Even then sometimes we wrap in a quilt and take it with us.

Uncle David and Nels have quilts on their beds, all-over pattern quilts made by my grandmother when she was old. The few times I've been in the room the beds were made all neat and square. Not like ours, which look like cattle have been jumping on them.

All over the walls are calendars and pictures. On Nels' side there are pictures of work horses in harness or just standing—big ones, Belgians and Percherons with their names written below them in pretty letters. There is also an old calendar from Norway, over twenty years old, with Norwegian writing on it that I can't understand and Wayne can't either. Though he sometimes says he can. Uncle David and Nels and Dad will talk Norwegian when they don't want us to understand, but it makes Mother mad—she can't speak Norwegian either—so they don't do it much.

It's as if there is a line drawn through the middle of the room. On one side is Nels and on the other side—in almost a different world—is

David. Where Nels has horses and cows and scenery, Uncle David has pictures of farm girls holding flowers and working in gardens, calendars with girls and horses on ranches out west—all of the girls blonde and pretty and smiling. Once I asked Father why Uncle David had so many pictures of girls and he said it was because he was once married to Alida but didn't have any pictures of her. When I asked him why Nels had no pictures of girls he said it was because Nels was never married. I don't know what he meant exactly, but many questions I ask Father are answered that way, with words around the edges.

Also on Uncle David's side of the room there are books. Not just the Bible. They both have the Bible by their beds. Father says they each read one verse to the other in Norwegian before they go to sleep. But on Uncle David's side there are four other books—only I don't know what they are because the titles and the writing are all in Norwegian. I know they're thick. Big books. Sometimes Uncle David will bring one of them down and read it in the kitchen at night because that's the only room with enough light. The Coleman lantern hangs in the middle of the room and hisses and gives off a flat light so bright you have to squint when you come in from the barn at night. Uncle David sits at the kitchen table and reads silently, his lips moving, sometimes for an hour and more. Once Wayne asked him what he was reading but he just shook his head and didn't answer. We knew it wouldn't do any good to ask after that. So we don't know what's in the books.

The rest of the farm is two granaries and a barn. The granaries are made of rough sawn wood polished smooth by all the oats and barley poured in and shoveled out for the stock. They sit one on each side of the farmyard to keep the wind from ripping through in the winter.

The barn is a large log building at the end of the yard. It has two floors, the upstairs being the hayloft, and is made of logs so big there aren't trees that large anymore. The bottom logs are so huge Wayne and I would have to link arms to get around one of them. The logs get smaller as the barn walls go up, because they had to be lifted, but the corners are linked and cut with wedge cuts so that as they settle they get tighter.

Wayne says the barn and house and granaries

were built before any of us came, even before Father's father came from the old country and died in the woods. I can't say it isn't so. Once I asked Father about it while we were waiting for hog water to heat for butchering which is the slowest of all times except Christmas Eve, waiting to fall asleep so you can get up and come down to see what's been left under the tree.

Father didn't know how old the farm was either, and when I asked Uncle David he just smiled and nodded and Nels didn't seem to hear me.

So the farm is old. Sometimes Wayne and I sit in the hayloft and wonder about the logs, about how old they are. You can see where the axes made marks when they were chopped and where the long drawknives made flat cuts when they were peeled, and in one log, near the end of the barn and down out of sight where you can barely see it, there is a name carved.

KARL, it says, in letters cut deep and so far under it had to have been done right after the tree was cut down. I asked Father and Nels and Uncle David and Mother and even Wayne, but none of them knew a Karl with a K, only several Carls that started with C. Somehow that made the name ancient. I saw Wayne sitting alone near the name touching it once with one finger and when I asked him what he was doing he just smiled.

That was the time, that spring, when Wayne and I went out in the woods near the backyard and found a large tree and carved our names in it. Wayne carved his in all large letters, using a wood chisel and a hammer, but I used a knife and didn't get mine so deep. I felt bad, until that winter Father cut the tree for pulp and sent it off to the paper mills where it would be shredded anyway. . . .

Inside the barn, the ground floor is laid out with a long aisle down the middle, where the cows are milked; on the right of that is a manger that runs the full length of the barn. The cows come in and put their heads through wooden slots called stanchions and Father or one of us goes down the line and closes them in with a locking board to hold their heads while we milk. Except in winter. In winter they stay in all the time because the deep cold is too much for them and they would die.

At the end of the manger area there is a little door cut in the wall that leads outside to a large covered pit full of silage. Silage is chopped corn and corn plants put up in the fall and fed to the cattle all winter. It is supposed to be good for them, and they love it and push against the stanchions and bellow when the small door is opened and they see Father come in with the silage fork. Uncle David says they do that because silage ferments and they get drunk on it. Either way, they eat every bit of it and lick the wood of the little silage box in front of each stanchion until the wood is shiny and as glass smooth as the salt block in the south pasture that they lick in the summer.

Across from the cows, on the other side of the barn, there is a row of calf pens. Each cow has to have a calf or it won't freshen and give milk. But the cow gives way more milk than even ten calves could drink so the calves are kept in a pen and fed milk with a bucket. The extra milk we keep for selling or drinking. There are three pens of calves and in the spring when they're born and put in the pens the barn is filled with the warm dampness of them. Uncle David calls it the best time there is, when the young come in the early spring. Sometimes he'll fill his lower lip with snoose and just stand by the pen, sucking on the tobacco and watching the calves quietly as they try to play and fall all over each other.

When the calves are brand new, they don't know how to drink out of a bucket and they run around the pen trying to suck on anything to get milk. They get each others' ears, or tails, or noses, or pieces of wood on the side of the barn. I saw one once get hold of a new kitten's tail and suck on it until the whole kitten was goobered with spit.

Wayne and I are the ones who get them to drink because our hands are smaller than the grown men's. When the milking is almost done we each take a small bucket of milk and climb into a calf pen. They're on you right away, sucking at your clothes or elbows and you have to get your fingers in their mouths and while each one is sucking on your fingers you pull your hand gently down into the warm milk and pretty soon they're sucking right at the milk and drinking it like they've known how all along. Unless they're dumb. Some of them are dumber than others and don't get it. Wayne had a calf two springs ago that never did learn, even when he got nearly big enough to be weaned. It was a sight, watching Wayne get into the pen with that huge calf. He would run over to Wayne and grab his hand and jerk it down into the bucket so he could get milk. It got so Wayne was half afraid to get into the pen and every morning when we came near to feeding calves he would start bargaining with me to take his calf.

"I'll let you read the Captain Marvel comic I got when we went to town Saturday."

"I already read it when you were sweeping the granary."

"I'll give it to you."

"I don't want to get into the pen with that calf."

"I'll give you that Captain Marvel and buy you one of those wax-teeth harmonicas when we go in with milk next Saturday. . . ."

"Nope."

I answered fast but it wasn't that easy a decision. Those orange wax teeth are something. You can play music on them for a while until you're sick of the squeaking sound they make that always causes Foursons, the dog, to cock his head sideways and look like the RCA dog on the radio in the pictures in the Sears catalog. Then you eat the wax, which has some sugar in it, and chew on it for hours and hours. And when that's done you give it to Foursons who eats it until he's sick of it and gives it to the chickens, who always follow him around hoping he'll drop something.

To be honest I thought if I held out I could maybe get a Coca Cola and a bag of peanuts to pour into it. Which I like better than the orange wax teeth.

Wayne was too tight and I didn't get any of it. He went ahead with the calf on his own even though when he climbed into the pen to feed it we all stopped our work to watch him.

On the same side of the barn as the calf pens, just at the end, is a separator room. All the milk has to have the cream taken out of it so the cream can be sold separately when we go in on Saturdays. Mother gets the cream money and egg money—and I guess all the money, come to think of it, because I saw Father turning over a check from the elevator for grain one fall, which is practically the only money we ever get. Milk and cream and egg and grain money.

The separator has a bowl on the top where we pour the milk and a crank on the side to turn it and spin the cream out. The crank is hard to turn until it gets going and then it's easy. But you have to keep turning it and turning it until all the milk's been run through, and sometimes they run it through twice.

Wayne and I have to turn the crank. He turns it one day and I turn it the next. We make marks on the wall with an old pencil stub to keep track of who's supposed to do it. We don't hate it, exactly, but like Wayne says if he had a choice between turning the separator or peeing on the weed-chopper electric fence he'd have to think about it a little and I agree with him.

Parts of it are nice, the separator. It makes a high whine, like you might have with a steam engine running; you can imagine that while you turn. And it's something to watch the cream come out one spigot, thick and rich, and the milk foam into the milk can out of the other one. It's all grass, Uncle David says, grass and corn. Wayne and I spent one whole day working out how we planted alfalfa and the cows ate it and we planted corn and the cows ate it and came into the barn and gave us milk for it which we sold to buy more alfalfa and corn seed to plant more to give them. . . .

"It's endless," Wayne said. "It just goes on and on and never ends. Like the stars and the weather."

"Unless all the cows get sick and die," I said, because I always disagree with Wayne and Wayne always disagrees with me.

"No good, Eldon," he said, shaking his head. "There's other cows and other corn and other alfalfa and other milk."

"Well, if all the cows died in all the places where there are cows it would end. Then the corn would rot and that would be the end of it."

Wayne didn't even answer. It was lame and I knew it, but it was all I could think of on short notice.

Next to the separator room is the work horses' stall. We have a team of two horses, Jim and Stacker, both geldings, so big Wayne and I have to climb their legs to help harness them. Their hooves are as large as pie plates. They stay in all winter except when they get used for hauling pulp wood on the big bobsleds or pull the stone-boat to clean the barn. Sometimes it's like they aren't real, Jim and Stacker—that's what Wayne says.

They are so big, so strong it's like they can't

be just horses. Father says they weigh close on a ton each but that doesn't mean much. It's the tallness of them. Sometimes in the barn we'll climb the stall sides and sit on the horses and talk because they are warm and gentle and somehow comfortable—like a living couch. One time we both got on Jim and sat on his rump, the two of us, and there was room to spare. It was like a huge fur table.

Come a late spring day maybe one, two years ago we went to town of a Saturday night so Father could have two beers—he always has two beers when he goes in with Mother to dance.

In the main room of the beer hall Harrin Olsen plays the accordion and does waltzes and polkas all night Saturday night. Harrin was kicked by a horse and can't talk or think much but he plays the accordion so wonderfully that people come from other towns just to hear him. And Mother and Father dance and dance. This one night he had his sleeves rolled up and clean overalls on and she was wearing a pretty flowered dress, and before you knew it everybody else had stopped to watch them twirl and twirl around the rough board floors of the beer hall. We watched till it

was boring and I left to go drink a Coca Cola
with peanuts in it and almost got in a fight with
Evan Peterson when he tried to take my Coca
Cola.

That night, in the back room, Wayne found a
Zane Grey western in a dusty pile. *Guns Along
the Powder River*. The cover was all in color and
showed a cowboy with a roaring six-gun in each
hand kind of shooting at you out of the picture.
So we sat down with that book and read it and
don't you know, we had to be cowboys. We
asked old man Engstrom, who owns the beer
hall, if we could borrow the book and he said
yes so we took it home.

It didn't happen all at once. We would read a
couple of pages and then we would pretend. We
had some sticks we used for blazing six-guns and
we would try to do whatever the cowboys in the
book were doing, and that was where Wayne
finally got into trouble. It was all right as long
as they were just shooting each other or gallop-
ing around. But we came to a scene where the
hero—he was named Jed—was being held in
the upstairs room in a ranch house by a gang of
rustlers who were stealing cattle. Jed had set out
to stop them, which he did with some pretty

good shooting, but that isn't so important. What matters is that for a while they captured him and held him in the upstairs room and the bad men were downstairs. So he whistled for Black Ranger, his horse, and Black Ranger came and stood under the back upstairs window and Jed jumped out of it and landed on Black Ranger and rode away and left the rustlers. Wayne thought it was quite the fancy thing to do.

"Why, I think it would be quite the fancy thing to do." That's how he said it.

But I was thinking more of the horse and what it must be like to have somebody jump out of an upstairs window and land on your back.

A few mornings later, Father and Mother went to Orvisons' for coffee because it was too soon to plant and they wanted to visit. Nels and Uncle David were in the house in their room and Wayne motioned for me to come with him to the barn.

"I want you to hold Stacker for me," he said, whispering so Uncle David and Nels wouldn't hear upstairs. "Underneath the hayloft door . . ."

I knew without being told what Wayne was going to do and I knew it was wrong but it didn't matter. I had to see him do it. Like the time he made wings out of some sticks and two feed sacks and tried to fly off the granary roof. A fool would know it wouldn't work, but I had to see it anyway and later, when they took the cast off his arm he was even kind of proud. He claimed he'd flown, but I thought and still think he came down like a rock with some rags tied to it.

The thing with Stacker was the same. The cowboy book had been chewing at him over a week so I followed him to the barn.

"I picked Stacker because he looks most like Black Ranger," he said as we went in. "To make it look right."

"The only thing that looks the same is that Stacker is a horse and kind of brown," I said. "He's got a leg that weighs more than Black Ranger. . . ."

Last year when Mother's cousin Betty was visiting with her daughter—this three-year-old girl who I guess would be my second cousin or something—anyway when they were visiting, the little girl got away from them while they were drinking coffee and talking. Everybody was frightened that she had wandered into the hog pen and the pigs had eaten her, which Nels and

Uncle David said had happened once when they were young. But we finally found the little girl in the pasture standing under Stacker. She was right between his front legs, holding onto the long hair around his hoofs, and when he'd step forward to move to a different piece of grass to eat—those feet as big as tree stumps swinging out so carefully to miss the little girl—she just moved with him, hanging onto his legs.

When we untied him and led him out of the stall—neither one of us coming up to his nose —he was just as easy and gentle as he'd been with the little girl.

"Are you sure you want to do this?" I asked. But I really wanted to see it and that came through in my voice. Like when Wayne tried to fly.

He just nodded and when we had Stacker out in front of the barn, under the hayloft door, he lined the horse up. That took some doing because Stacker had no idea what he was supposed to be there for, standing waiting for a make-believe cowboy to jump out of the sky onto his back, so he kept trying to move. We'd stop him just right, then he'd take a step to eat the thistles at the edge of the barn and ruin it. We went back and forth until finally Stacker seemed to get the idea and he stood.

"You hold him right here," Wayne said, "and I'll get up in the hayloft"—as if I would be the one to get in the hayloft.

He ran into the barn and I heard him thumping up the hayloft ladder and in a few seconds he opened the loft door over Stacker.

He looked down for a moment and held back. "It's pretty far. . . ."

The truth is I kind of agreed with him, but I didn't say anything. My job was to hold Stacker. Period.

Finally he shrugged. "Well, if Jed could do it . . ."

Then Wayne turned around and said back into the empty barn, "Don't worry. I'll be back with the posse," like Jed to his sidekick.

And he jumped.

I'm not sure how he figured the drop from the hayloft to Stacker. I know that when Jed did it in the book he jumped out of the window and landed perfectly in the saddle and rode away just as clean and nice as you could hope for and not a rustler knew he was leaving.

It didn't work out that way for Wayne. Of course Stacker wasn't wearing a saddle, but even if he had been, Wayne wouldn't have come anywhere close to it. Wayne had judged the distance all wrong and Stacker's front end was way out from the barn. That put his rear end directly under the hayloft opening.

Wayne hit with a sound kind of like smacking a potato with a hammer.

Chunnkks.

It must have hurt because when I looked up at his eyes all that showed were the whites, and he slowly rolled off the side of Stacker and plopped into the manure and muck on the ground and didn't move but just lay still holding himself down there making a kind of whistling sound through his nose.

Stacker is a soft and slow-moving old horse. Many times I've seen Father take a carrot and hold it in his mouth and Stacker will pluck it out without hurting a hair on Father's head. But Stacker had never had anybody jump out of a hayloft and land on his rump, and when Wayne hit him Stacker jumped forward. He moved really fast for a big horse. The jump took him into the side of the pig fence, which knocked the boards down. All the pigs—about four months old—saw the hole and went for it, which took them right across Wayne, who was still down on the ground whistling.

I couldn't help him at first because I'd been trying to hold Stacker by his halter, which was about the same as trying to hold a train. He didn't even feel me when he jumped forward. Then I looked back and saw Wayne on the ground with the little pigs running over him, holding himself and his eyes all white and the wind whistling out of his nose, and I started laughing so hard I couldn't stop. It just got worse and worse until I was hanging on the side of the hog fence and I guess I'd be hanging there still if Wayne hadn't gotten better and come after me with an old board.

He's still sore about it. All I've got to do to get his eyes glowing is look at him and say, "Don't worry. I'll be back with the posse."

SUMMER

Summer starts slow. You don't really see the work coming. One day it's spring, soft and sticky and stinking and the hard part of winter is done and you walk around looking for something to do. The next day Father is taking the plowshares to town. The soil on the back forty is rocky and dulls the cutting edge of the plow—the shares— and every year the blacksmith has to hammer them out to a sharp edge again.

Plowing is the only time Father uses the F-12. That's our tractor and it's quite a sight, with steel lug wheels and a crank start, and so ornery only Father can get it going. Even with him it's mean. Two summers ago he had the spark from the magneto too far advanced and the crank kicked back and broke his wrist. He had to wear a cast half of a summer.

Father used to use the team for plowing, riding the one-bottom plow and letting them make their own speed. But on a warm day he would have to stop and water them and let them rest at each end of the field. When he had a chance to swap two Jerseys for the tractor he did it. Mother was upset though because she liked the milk from the Jerseys better than from the Holsteins. It had more cream to it, she said, and it tasted better.

I like taking the plowshares into town with Father because I'm still young enough to go. Wayne has crossed the line now and has to work around the farm when he isn't going to school. Unless it's Saturday night in the spring, Wayne has to stay home. But I still get to climb into the old Ford truck with the cable brakes and ride with Father to town.

The blacksmith is a tall, thin man smelling of burned steel and snoose spit. We leave the plowshares there to be worked on and Father takes me to the store where I get a nickel every time and spend it on candy that costs two for a penny. It's rock-hard candy and I'm supposed to save some for Wayne. Sometimes I do, but usually I suck all of mine and some of Wayne's before I get home, and to be honest the candy is mostly why I like to come to town.

Once I asked Father why he didn't take the shares in during the winter or even spring and do it then. He said it was because the steel would forget it was sharp if it wasn't done right before early plowing. But he was smiling so I don't know about it being true and I'm afraid to ask Wayne because he would laugh at me for sounding dumb.

When the shares are heated red hot and pounded out to a new edge with the big hammer we take them home and Father bolts them onto the bottom edge of the plow to cut the soil. Then he hooks the plow to the tractor and heads for the fields.

I have to wait for Mother and walk out with her when she brings lunch to him. She takes sandwiches in a covered bucket with a quart jar full of coffee wrapped in sacking to keep it hot and two or three pieces of cake and some large pickles from last year's garden. We sit at the end of the field and wait for Father to finish his round, the tractor popping and snapping in the heat. Then he gets down and we sit in the shade to eat. Mother spreads one of the sacks from around the coffee on the ground as a tablecloth and puts out the sandwiches and cake and brushes the flies away with a hand while we eat. Father talks about how the soil is.

"She's butter," he says sometimes. "Just a little moisture this spring and she's cutting like butter. I've never seen the beat. . . ."

And when lunch is done, some days he'll let me ride on the tractor with him and watch the plow. Father says that is the best part of farming—plowing in the early summer—and I can see why he thinks it. I think the same.

The plow turns the soil, just peels it and turns it over so the bright green of the grass is folded and folded and folded under and the thick black of the soil turns up. I like to sit backward on the tractor seat and watch.

Then the seagulls come. Father says they come from large lakes to the north and maybe from Hudson's Bay which is north many hundreds of miles. He says that when he was young there were no gulls but they discovered the plowing one year and the next year they came and each year now they come.

Hundreds of them. They come to float in back of the tractor and watch, and each time the plow turns over a worm they drop down to pick it up and eat it. They float in rows and piles and heaps in the air around the tractor and plow and you would think they'd fight but they don't. No fighting. They take turns. They will hang on the air like thistledown, soft and easy, and when a worm turns up one will drop down and nail it and another will take his place, so that they seem to turn, gray and white gulls, as the soil turns over and over. It would be much prettier if they didn't poop so much.

It drops on your head and in your face and on the tractor and plow and the hot muffler on the engine. The stink burns and cuts back across the tractor seat in a thick cloud. Father says it is a rich smell, and he loves the gulls, but to me it just stinks. To Wayne it stinks. Nels and Uncle David won't say if it stinks or smells nice when I ask them. And Mother just smiles when I ask her.

Once the plowing is done, Father puts the tractor away and uses Stacker and Jim to pull the disc harrow to break the soil down still more. Then, when it is in small lumps, he drags the toothed drag with the team over it one more time and breaks it down further until it's like cake batter. That's how Father says it. He'll feel the dirt and sometimes take a pinch up and taste it and smile at me if I'm sitting on the drag or harrow with him and say, "It's smooth as cake batter."

Of course it isn't. But he's always doing that, saying things are like something else to make you think about them. Like Stacker and Jim pulling stumps when he's clearing the forty down by the swamp. That's something to see, almost to not believe—how strong they are and how they'll still let me climb their legs like trees.

Father backs them up to the stump so the doubletree—the joining bar you use on a two-horse team—is on the ground next to it. Then he wraps a short chain under the stump and hooks it to the doubletree and he says, ever so soft, "Jim. Stacker. Take it up."

They pull and their leg muscles snap and crack so hard sometimes on a warm day that the sweat sprays off those horses in a fine mist. The trace chains and doubletree creak and the stump hangs for a minute, then pop! like my old tooth in back when Mother used a string on it, pop!

that old stump comes out in a shower of dirt and Stacker and Jim lunge forward a bit with the pull before they can stop.

"Did you see their legs, boy?" Father says. "Like pistons, weren't they? Like pistons on a big engine when they snap like that . . ."

But they aren't. They're just strong meat. That's what Wayne says. But he never says it in front of Father and besides, in the summer, Wayne is working so hard there isn't time to say much of anything.

Uncle David once said it was because there was so much light in the summer.

"You work in light," he said, sitting on a cream can by the barn door, spitting in the dust so the chickens came running to see what it was. "With all the summer light it makes us work harder. In winter it gets dark earlier and the days are short enough to rest. No rest in the summer."

And sometimes Uncle David is never wrong so that might be the way of it.

I can't work all the hard ways Father and Uncle David and Nels and even Wayne work because when I was small I had a time when I couldn't quit coughing. I spit blood and was weak for what seemed forever, and now I'm supposed to take it easy until I get older. I can play hard with Wayne and it doesn't seem to bother me. But Mother and Father won't let me do the hard work like clean the barn or shovel grain or even carry wood, even though I do it when they aren't watching.

First there is plowing, then dragging and harrowing and drilling the seed: wheat, oats, barley, corn—then potatoes; and the days don't stop. Father leaves the milking to the rest of us, or I should say everybody but me, and takes Stacker and Jim out of the stalls before light. He leaves so far before light that Mother doesn't even have a chance to get breakfast for him; he just eats some cold food from supper the night before. I got up one morning and went out in my shorts with rubber boots on and watched him when he didn't see me. He talked so nice to Jim and Stacker in the dark that it was like they weren't horses but good friends.

"We got corn," he said, his voice even and steady as he hooked them to the corn planter. "Got corn to put in and we got to lay those rows so straight they be like a die, straight as a die they got to be. . . ." All the words ran together and you could hear the horses whicker to him in a kind of answer while he fastened the trace chains and raised the tongue between them to slip into the tongue ring. Then it was just the three of them as he climbed onto the planter and rode out of the yard, clucking to the team to keep them going. I thought then and still think that when he is with them working that way, Father loves those horses every bit as much as he loves Mother or Wayne or me or anything.

"Work on work on work"—that's how Uncle David says it.

When the corn is planted and comes up it has to be cultivated three or four times to make sure the weeds don't get a start. And about when the corn cultivating is done and the plants are standing alone and free of weeds it's time to do hay.

That's when the neighbors, the Ransens, come, like they do in harvest time; when they hay, we go to help them. But it's a lot of work, even with help. The hay has to be mowed, then raked into winrows and dried, then swept up with the sweeprakes and brought to the hay stackers that pull the piles of hay up and over the top again and again to make the stacks. I even get to do some work at haying time. When the hay comes up and over to fall on top of the stack, two of us—Wayne and I—have to use three-tined hay forks to smooth the hay and shape it so it sheds water down the outside of the stack. It also has to be packed, so we jump on it and bounce it down after the sweeprake teams bring in each new pile, until all the hay for winter is in stacks in the field looking like loaves of bread.

Just about when haying is done it's time to thrash. That's Father's favorite time if there's been good rain and the oats and wheat are good, and his sad time if it's been dry and the oats and wheat didn't make right.

We also thrash with the Ransens, except it's different from haying. When we hay everybody works and when the day is done we all go home to finish work at home. But when we thrash we don't go home right away. We cut the grain and use the shaulker to put it in bundles and feed it to the thrashing machine which is run by the F-12 and a long, slapping belt. Grain comes out a spout at the top and straw comes out the other end and dust, eye-dust, choke-dust, sneeze-dust, is all over the place so the men have to wear handkerchiefs over their noses just to breathe.

When we're done we wash in the water trough in back of the barn where you can also catch tadpoles if you want to put some in a jar. But instead of everybody going home, all the men and women stay and eat. There's never food like there is at thrashing. At our house Mother cooks all of a day just on pies, then all of a night, it seems, on meat and potatoes and all of the next day on all the other things there are to eat. Everybody brings something as well, and a table is made outside with planks covered with clean sheets.

I don't know how men can eat like that. Old man Ransen, who they say is close on seventy, always comes—even though he doesn't do any work except oil the thrasher now and then with an oil squirt can. That makes Uncle David mad because he thinks he should do it. Old man Ransen sets to and the gravy runs down his chin. He eats like six young men, even without teeth. I watched him last year during thrashing finish off four plates of food, half an apple pie, and close on a quart of homemade ice cream that Wayne and I had spent hours cranking. And then he looked for more.

It's something to see. Wayne and I just eat and

eat until we're close to busting and there's still so much food left the table almost creaks with it.

When the thrashing is done there's a mountain of straw out in back of the barn where the thrashing machine blows it; Wayne and I sometimes spend a whole day jumping off the barn roof onto the straw pile, even though there's the second cutting of hay to get in and the corn silage to chop. I think Father knows how much we still like to jump in the straw and just lets us have the day for it. Once I saw him and Mother watching us from the side of the granary as we jumped, and they were both laughing and looked like they wanted to jump with us. I think you could jump from the clouds and it wouldn't hurt if you landed in a straw pile. You just sink and sink and sink. . . .

Then hay again, and corn to fill the silo to feed the cattle all winter—and how hard it is. Maybe I wouldn't have known, except that last year at the end of summer I came around the end of the barn and saw Father sitting on the block of oak we use for splitting wood and killing chickens. He was just sitting looking at the ground with his hands and arms hanging down between his legs. His eyes weren't blinking and he wasn't smiling. Mother was standing in back of him rubbing his shoulders and neck, just rubbing and rubbing.

"The days are long," she said, in a kind of song like she used to sing to me when the coughing was bad and I couldn't sleep. "The days are long and the nights are short, the days are long and the nights are short. . . ."

Many times we eat supper after ten, when it is dark, the Coleman lantern hissing and nobody talking, nobody saying anything, even Wayne and me, just eating and chewing and eating until we're done and then we go up to fall in our beds for the next day.

Summer work.

You swear it will never end until one day, one hot day in September Father will head out in the morning and harness Jim and Stacker to the hayrack and look at us and say, "Pile on, we're going to the lake."

Then you know it's fall.

FALL

I hate fall.

Mother says it's her favorite time and Nels and Uncle David like it because the air starts to dry out and they don't ache so much. Father seems to walk lighter. All the grain is up and the barn is full of hay and the fields are tucked in with haystacks waiting to be used and everything is done. Almost everything.

Going to the lake starts it off better than it ends. I like that part. Three miles away over a logging road is a small lake called Jenny's Lake because a girl was supposed to have killed herself there when the man she was going to marry died in the war. I don't know which war it was, but it's supposed to be true. Wayne says her ghost walks on the water in the dark sometimes, but he's never been there in the dark and neither have I, so there's no way to know for sure.

It's a pretty lake. Almost perfectly round with a small beach and a grassy place at one end where Father long ago—when he came there with Mother while they were courting—made a rock fireplace. In a tree at the edge of the clearing he carved their initials in a heart. They are still there, the bark grown around them so they look old and deep. Once I saw Mother go over to the tree, two, three falls ago, and put her fingers on the heart and smile and look at Father who was making a fire to cook the steaks.

We always make a fire and he lets it burn down to coals and cooks steaks on a grill. Or pork chops. Mother brings pies and potato salad and jars of raspberry drink she makes from the raspberry syrup she saves when she cans. We eat until we can't hold any more. Then Wayne and I get in the water at the beach and spend the afternoon swimming and splashing while Mother and Father and Nels and Uncle David sit on the grass and look across the lake and burp and smile and talk about silly things that don't go together. . . .

"Was a time when you couldn't move in this country," Uncle David might say. "Trees so thick you couldn't move at all. . . ."

"Sure good food," Father would answer, looking straight at Mother who would blush and blush. "For somebody so pretty. I didn't think pretty women could cook that good."

"I had a mare once," Nels might say, "that every time you slapped her she peed straight back like a bullet. Got Hans—you remember Hans, don't you, the one that got killed when the tree hit him? Got him straight in the ear and he was so mad he hit me with a peavy. . . . But he never got earaches again as long as he lived."

. . . Until it's close to evening and we eat warm apple pie and drink milk thick with cream and barely make it home in time to milk and do chores. That's how fall starts.

Not so bad a start.

But when all the grain is up and all the silage in and the hay stacked and the barn and yard cleaned it is time to kill.

And I don't like the killing part.

We have a dog named Rex that's been here longer than Wayne. He's got hair in lumps and likes to help bring the cows in, but he's so old he mostly just sits and stinks on the porch and thumps his tail if you say his name or hand him a pork-chop bone. Father says Rex stopped a bear that was chasing Mother from the garden before we were born and that's why he only has to sit on the porch and eat.

But come fall he goes crazy. It's the blood, Father says. As soon as Father walks out of the house and takes the little .22 rifle down from the old deer horns on the porch to shoot the steer, Rex gets to jumping and wheezing so hard he almost chokes.

I think he's the only one on the place that likes the killing.

It's the way of it, Father says. Something has to die so we can live. Mother nods but she doesn't come out to the barn, only when the killing is done and the skinning and cutting start.

It's one of those things I wish I didn't watch but I do. Wayne says that makes me two-faced but I can't help it. Father goes into the barn with the little rifle and holds it to the steer's head and pops it once and the steer goes down, just flumps down, and then Father cuts the throat with the curved knife and catches the blood in a large pan for mother to make blood sausage out of. I can't eat it, ever, but that's not the worst.

Then he and Uncle David and Nels use a pulley and rope to pull the steer up to the ceiling in the barn and cut the belly open, the knife sliding through it like butter, and all the guts drop down in blue coils with steam off them, but that's not the worst.

Even when Rex jumps in and starts to eat the guts and gets them all over his head, and the cats come down from the hayloft and eat at them with the funny sideways grin they have when they eat guts, and the smell makes me a little sick and I have to go outside and breathe on the sides of my tongue—that's not the worst.

The pigs are the worst.

When I was sick and couldn't play hard and coughed blood, I sometimes got hot at night, so hot I couldn't stand it and I would have dreams.

Because of the blood I coughed up I dreamt of blood. And *my* throat. And the dream has never really gone away, because sometimes I wake up even now and my eyes will be wide open and Mother will have to come in and put her hand on my head.

Blood and throats.

When Father kills a pig he doesn't shoot it like he does with a steer because he says pigs have to bleed out better.

He uses the curved knife, and the men put the pig in the same pen they used for the steer. Then they flip the pig on his back and Nels and Uncle David hold him while Father sticks the curved knife into the pig's throat. And the throat seems to jump at it, seems to pull the knife in and up in a curve to cut its big vein. And the pig screams and screams while it dies and bleeds out. The smell, the smell of the blood and the screams and the throat bleeding out is so much, so thick that I can't stand it.

There is more killing in the fall: The chickens have to be killed and canned for winter—killed with the ax so their heads lop off and the beaks open and close even though the heads aren't on the bodies and the bodies jump around and around with Rex chasing them as they splatter blood on the barn wall from their jumping— bright specks of new blood on the walls of the barn that looks like the blood I coughed up. And there's the stink of their feathers as they are dipped in hot water and plucked, Wayne and Mother and me plucking them, pulling the damp, stinking feathers out, even working close around the stump of the neck.

Then the two geese we get from Hemings every year to smoke and save for Christmas have to be killed and plucked and waxed and smoked and they stink and there is blood and blood and blood and more blood and I hate fall.

By the end of it, by the end of fall, all I know is blood and if it weren't for school to think about I couldn't stand it. I know it has to be done, and every year Mother explains it to me again, though she doesn't come to the barn when the killing happens. I can't help thinking it's wrong, though Wayne doesn't think so. Sometimes he seems to get a light in his eyes like Rex gets when Father kills. But the men don't like it, Uncle David and Nels don't like it because when Father kills the steer and it goes down and when he cuts the hog and it screams and bleeds to death, when that is done Nels and Uncle David always stand silently, take their caps off and stand silently until it is done.

And Father always turns away and spits after he has done it. Nobody says anything for a time while the animals or chickens are dying. Nothing. No sound and I hate fall.

WINTER

Wayne says there aren't any divisions in things. We had a big fight one time over whether or not there was a place between days when it wasn't the day before and it wasn't tomorrow yet. I said there were places, divisions in things so you could tell one from the next but he said no there wasn't and we set to it. By the time we were done I had a bloody nose and he had a swollen ear from where I hit him with a board and we still didn't know.

But there is a place where winter comes, a place to see it isn't fall any longer and know winter is here.

When the killing is done and the meat is up and the crops are in and the leaves have all gone to color and dropped off the trees and the gray limbs stick up like ugly fingers; when the barn is scraped clean inside and straw is laid for the first cold-weather bedding and the stock tank in back of the barn has ice on it that has to be broken in the mornings so the horses can drink; when you have to put choppers on your hands to fork hay down from the loft to the cows and the end of your nose gets cold and Rex moves into the barn to sleep and Father drains all the water out of all the radiators in the tractors and the old town truck and sometimes you suck a quick breath in the early morning that is so cold it makes your front teeth ache; when the chickens are walking around all fluffed up like white balls and the pigs burrow into the straw to sleep in the corner of their pen, and Mother goes to Hemings for the quilting bee they do each year that lasts a full day—when all that happens, fall is over.

But it still isn't winter.

When all the fall things are done there is the place between that Wayne says isn't so but is. There is something there and when we come out of the barn sometimes I can feel it. A sort of quiet. Once I stopped Wayne just as we were walking to the barn and it was getting dark and the clouds were sailing over our heads heading south and there was a north wind so you had to hold your head over into your collar to keep your ear warm; once then I stopped Wayne and asked him if he could feel it.

"Feel what?"

"Feel the place between," I said, and he looked at me and said he thought maybe I was crazy like those natives we read about in *National Geographic* who would predict weather and fall down.

But I didn't care and don't care now because I know the place is there. The place when fall is gone and winter hasn't come yet. It is a short time, in one night.

And then it snows.

First time.

You go to bed after chores and when you wake up and go downstairs and the sun starts to come up there is a new light to it, a brighter light; you look out the window and there is new snow all over everything.

First snow.

Soft and curved and white covering the yard and dirt and manure and grass and old leaves, the barns and granaries and machines out by the small tool shed, so that they don't look like buildings and machines at all but animals. White animals in the new light.

First snow.

Winter.

And winter isn't like any of the other parts of the year more than any other part isn't. Spring is close to summer, summer close to fall, but winter stands alone. That's how Uncle David says it. Back in the old country he said winter stood alone and now he says it stands alone here as well.

Winter comes in one night and of course Wayne and I look out the window in the morning and there are a million snow things to do.

After chores we take the grain shovels and slide down the river hill sitting on them, holding the handles up and trying to steer by pushing them. The first time they move kind of slow, but when the snow is packed they just fly down. We can't really steer them at all but just snort and whistle down the hill until we get so wet that Mother makes us come in and change.

Then we have to make snow forts and throw snowballs at each other. And the chickens. All fluffed and looking for a warm place to stand. If they come too close to the fort they get it, or Rex, or the cats, or anything.

. . . All the snow things to do. Father feels it too. One winter he hooked Stacker to a singletree with a rope out the back, and we stood on a piece of old tin roofing with a rope tied to it and we rode and rode, the tin so slick Stalker didn't know it was there. Big as he was the cold snapped him up and he acted like a colt, if colts can get as big as barns, just snorting and flipping his tail and making air, whipping that piece of tin and us all over the field in the snow until we were so cold and sopping that we were sticking to the tin.

Winter is all changes. Snow comes and makes it all different outside so things you see in the other times of the year are covered and gone. In back of the house there is an old elm that has a long sideways limb and one warm day some of the snow melted a bit and slipped down and then refroze so it looked like a picture of a snake we saw once in a magazine, or so Uncle David said. At night I could look out the bedroom window and see the snake hanging in the moonlight, the white snake and it seemed to move. It wasn't there in the summer or spring or fall but only in the winter. Like magic.

But finally, when the snow play is done and the barn and animals are settled in and the wood for the day finished, when our mittens are drying on the back of the kitchen stove and we have eaten the raw fried potatoes and strips of flank meat with the Watkins pepper on them and had the rhubarb sauce covered with separated cream, sitting at the kitchen table with the lantern hissing over our heads, finally when our stomachs are full Father pushes his chair away from the table and thanks Mother and God for the food and moves into the winter room. The living room.

Wayne and I have to do the dishes, and that includes washing the separator, which takes a long time, so when we get into the winter room the fire in the stove has been freshened with white oak and Mother is sitting knitting socks and mittens, and Father sits on one side of the stove and Uncle David sits on the other, with Nels next to him.

While Father has been filling the stove Mother has lighted the kerosene lamp so there is a soft yellow glow in the room. Wayne and I sit on the rug that Mother sewed out of braided rags, the colors all wrapped together in the soft light so they seem to move.

Father is working on his carving. I don't know when he started it. Maybe before I was born. But for as long as Wayne and I can remember he has been working at it every night in the winter. It will be a carving of a team of horses and a sleigh and trace chains and harnesses and reins and a man driving with a full load of pulp logs on the sleigh—all carved out of one piece of sugar-white pine he cut from a clear log many years ago. All we can see is the two horses' heads sticking out and part of one front shoulder, but Father can tell us where each thing is, pointing to where the links of chain will be and the logs and the man's head, just like he can see them even when they aren't there.

He carves quietly, his face even and somehow gentle, looking down as the small knife he uses cuts into the soft pine to peel away shavings so clear they look like honey in the yellow light from the lamp.

Wayne and I watch the fire in the stove through the mica windows in the door—all little squares—and the stove is like a friend. In the summer it is black and large and fills the corner of the room but now it is warm and part of us somehow. It is tall and narrow, and on top there is a silver ornament that looks like a big rose upside down. Around the side there is a silver rail that Wayne says is to put your feet on to warm them. But one night when nobody was looking I sneaked a spit on the rail and it snapped and sizzled like I'd spit on the top of the stove where it gets red, so I'm not about to stick a foot on that rail.

Next to the stove, across from Father, sits Uncle David and right next to him sits Nels. The two old men have straight-backed wooden chairs and a couple of old coffee cans they use for spitting into. They both fill their lower lip with snoose after we eat, and they sit straight up in the chairs, and Nels doesn't say anything except to slap his leg now and again when a story gets good.

Every night in the winter it starts the same. Uncle David and Nels will fill their lower lips and Father will carve and Mother will knit and the yellow flames will make our faces burn, and then Uncle David will spit in the coffee can

and rub his hands on his legs and take a breath
and say:

"It was when I was young. . . ."

Then he will tell the story of Alida who was
his wife in the old country. Always it is the same.
Always he tells the story of Alida first and it is
the same story.

∽ ALIDA

"It was when I was young and was thought fit only to sharpen the tools of the older men. This was wrong, wrong then and wrong now, but that is the way they did things in the old country. So each day I sat in front of the cottage and drew the stone over the axes and filed the saws until there was only new steel and the axes could shave the hair off your arm.

. "It was when I was young and a day came when a girl walked by as I was sharpening tools and she was so beautiful she made my tongue stick to the roof of my mouth and I could not speak. Yellow hair she had, yellow hair like cornsilk mixed with sunlight. It was so long she had it coiled in a braid at the back of her head. And her eyes were clear blue. Ice blue. She was carrying a towel filled with loaves of bread to take to the cutters in the woods and she stopped and said good day to me and I could not answer.

"Could not answer.

"And that was Alida. She became my wife and let her hair down for me in great coils in the light from tallow candles. I could not live without her. We were married there in the old country and I put the handkerchief on my head to show I would be a good husband. I grew from sharpening tools to using an ax and a bucksaw and we planned to come to America, planned and saved. But soon Alida was with child and we had to stay and when the child came it was a wrong birth and the child died and Alida died and I died.

"I wandered into the woods along Nulsek Fjord, walked in the snow and wind and would not have come back except that my brother Nels came for me and found me and brought me with him to America to work where there was new wood to cut and woods that go to the sky. But I never remarried and never looked at another woman and my heart has never healed, and that is the story of Alida.''

Uncle David always starts with the story of Alida. He has told it so often that when it comes out there aren't many stops except that his voice always hitches when he talks about Alida letting her hair down in the light from the tallow candles and I can see her so plain, so plain, and Mother always cries.

Father makes a small cough like there was something in his throat and Wayne takes a deep breath and Nels looks at the floor and doesn't move and Mother always cries and it is quiet— so quiet when he finishes the story of Alida that it seems as if time has stopped and we are all back with her and the bread in towels and Uncle David sharpening the tools of the older men.

Then Uncle David sighs and rubs his hands on his trouser leg and leans over to spit in the can and starts the second story of the night. The other stories are all different, always different night after night through the winter, so many stories I can't know them all or say them all.

But three of them I know.

Three of the stories make cuts across all the

stories the way a bucksaw cuts across wood so you can see all the rings and know how old the tree is, so you can know all about the tree.

Three are the stories like rings and show how it was that Wayne, and maybe me a little, came close to ruining it all, killing it all.

So Uncle David sits and he spits in the can and rubs his legs with hands callused so thick they look like bone or wood and he sighs and starts each one the same.

~ ORUD THE TERRIBLE

"It was when I was young that Siggurd came to me and told me the story of Orud and the house under the sea.

"The story was from old times, when men went off in long boats and many did not come back and those who did had blood on their bodies and blood on their swords and blood in their hearts.

"Men took then, and did not give so much but took what they wanted. The man who took the most was Orud. Orud was tall and wide in the shoulder and had a helmet made of steel hammered to a point but soaked in salt until it was red, red like blood. They called him Orud the Red when they went a-viking and he was so terrible that it was said even the men in his boat feared him, and these men feared nothing.

"So it came that on one voyage they went to far shores where they had not been before. They found small houses along the shore which were not rich in gold but all had much in livestock and wool and flax and wheat, and Orud and his men went among them and took and took and killed and killed until their arms were tired with it and they had to stop.

"Orud had never taken a wife. But on this voyage in one of the houses along the sea his men found a woman of beauty and her name was Melena. Orud decided to claim her for a wife, which was his right as he was captain of the boat.

"But such was Melena's beauty, with long, red-gold hair to match the color of burnished steel and a straight back and long arms, such was her beauty that the man who found her wanted her as his own wife and claimed her, and that was his right as well.

"But Orud would not have Melena go to another man. So they fought and the other man was weaker, as all men were weaker than Orud, and the other man lost and was slain. Orud put his head on an oar to boast and would not even bury the man as his station demanded. It was an awful thing then, to kill one of your own men and not even give him a Viking funeral, but they set sail with good wind to head home. Orud tied Melena in the bow of the longboat so she could not escape.

"But she was more than beautiful. Melena was smart and strong, and she waited until the boat was entering the fjord of Orud's home village and they could hear the horns sounding, waited until all could see the boat and see her. Then she stood on the side and used her magic to release her bonds and threw herself into the water rather than be wed to Orud.

"Such was Orud's rage when she leaped that he forgot himself and jumped after her, to bring her back.

"But he forgot he was wearing armor and his sword and helmet to be welcomed with his new wife. The weight took him down into the deeps and he was not seen again.

"Except that much bad came to the village. The people had sickness and their crops died and when they tried to go a-viking to make up for it their boats sank again and again.

"It was said that Orud had found Melena and taken her to be his wife though she did not want it, and that they lived in a cottage under the sea at the mouth of the fjord but that Melena had not forgiven the village for sending the boat which carried Orud to take her. It was said she cursed the village into sickness and waste and when she looked up and saw the village send out a boat she would spread her hair up from the bottom in long strands and catch the boat and sink it in vengeance and laugh at Orud, and the wind and waves were her laughter, and that is the story of Orud and Melena and the house beneath the sea."

The night of that story we sat quietly and thought of the cottage under the water and Melena's hair streaming up to gather in the boats, and Orud's terrible rage. Then Uncle David sighed and spit again and held his hands to the stove for the warmth. Mother shook her head thinking of the horror of Orud, and Nels coughed, and Uncle David gave a little chuckle and told the story of Crazy Alen.

CRAZY ALEN

"It was when I was still young but I had come to the new country and I was cutting in the woods.

"We were cutting in a camp called Folter, on the line between two counties then. I had a way with a file so they paid me extra to sharpen the saws at night and at times during the day. Because of that I was in camp many times when the other men were out cutting and so I knew more of the story of Crazy Alen than many of them.

"Alen came years before I did, came on a boat from the old country just as I did but long ago when they had to sail. He wasn't crazy at first but cut wood better than many men and was fast. He used a bucksaw and would pull so hard he often pulled the man on the other end off his feet, and the sawdust would fly out in a plume.

"But a day came when he started to play jokes on the other men in the camp. They were not bad jokes, didn't hurt anybody, and many laughed at them and that made him do all the more. He would put pepper in their snoose or sew their stockings closed or nail a board over the hole in the outhouse.

"He was finally known for his humor and the jokes became larger until one day he waited until the foreman—he disliked the foreman then—was in the outhouse and Alen dropped a Norway pine so big you couldn't reach around it, dropped it right in front of the door so close the foreman couldn't get out. It was the best of all his jokes, dropping the tree that close to the door, and took great skill. Trees don't always drop where they are supposed to drop. Everybody thought it very funny.

"Everybody except the foreman, who saw only the danger in it. Had the tree dropped a little to the side it would have crushed the whole outhouse with the foreman inside it.

"And so it came that the foreman fired Alen

—they called him Crazy Alen by this time, because of his jokes—but Alen didn't mind. He was getting old by then and had decided to stop work and watch things for a while. He made himself a small cabin on the side of a narrow trail back in the forest.

"In the way these things work Alen and the foreman then became good friends. Part of it was that the foreman was also old and most of the rest of the crew was young; and part of it was that the foreman missed Alen's jokes and humor. He could not hire Alen back to work, because somebody might be hurt, but the foreman began to like Alen's jokes himself and one day he walked into the cabin with some honey in a bucket he'd stolen from the camp cook and a checkerboard.

"Soon he was walking back along the narrow trail once a week to play checkers and drink tea with honey and this went on through part of a winter, a spring, a summer and fall and into winter again. The two men would sit and drink tea and play checkers and speak of things they'd done when they were young, and not so young, in that small cabin in the forest.

"Of course Alen's jokes hadn't stopped. Every

time the foreman came to play checkers Alen would have a new one, a bigger joke. He would have a bucket of water over the door with a trip lever set to drop when the foreman came in. Or he would loosen the rungs in the foreman's chair so it would collapse when he sat down. Or he would put salt in his tea. Since all of these jokes were aimed at the foreman you'd think he would get mad but things were different then, different and maybe a little rough, and so men didn't mind rough jokes and the foreman didn't mind Alen.

"Nobody can know how long it would have gone on, but that winter Alen felt death coming and decided to play his best joke of all. As a young man he had been big, big and heavy. Alen stood six-and-a-half feet and weighed two hundred and seventy pounds at least in his prime and his arms were long and heavy as well. He had come in and down with age, but the frame was still there and it was a big frame.

"In the middle of that winter when it was so cold you could spit and it would bounce, when steel ax heads broke if they weren't warmed before you chopped, in that cold Alen saw his death coming.

"Nobody knew how he could have done it,

but just before he died he opened the cabin door to let the cold in and lay down on the floor on his back with his arms and legs stretched out as wide open as he could get them. And then he died.

"He died with a wide smile on his lips and his arms and legs out and his eyes staring wide open at the ceiling.

"And it was in the middle of the week and four days passed before the foreman came to play checkers. Four days with the door open Alen lay and the cold came into the room and the cold came into Alen and froze him as hard as granite. Then the foreman came and found him spread and solid on the floor.

"Alen knew these things. He knew the cabin had a small door and that the trail down through the woods was narrow and winding and he knew the foreman. He knew the foreman wouldn't be able to bring himself to break Alen's arms and legs and he knew the foreman would not dare to thaw Alen because of what would get soft with the thaw.

"He knew these things, Alen did, and he knew one more thing, knew the foreman would not leave the body. Could not leave the body.

"And so it was his greatest joke on the foreman because Alen would not fit through the door. The foreman had to use an ax to cut the door opening wider and then try to get Alen—spread and hard and smiling—get Alen down the trail. It was nearly impossible. He tried to carry Alen but he was too heavy. He tried to drag him. Finally he tried to roll him, cartwheel him, and where tree limbs were too low he used an ax to chop a way through.

"Two days and a night it took him to get Alen's body back to the camp. Two days wheeling and dragging and carrying the spread-eagled man and when he finally got to camp they put Alen in the back of a sleigh and it took two more days to get him to town and an undertaker. It was said that as the sleigh went down the road all those who saw Alen thought he was waving and they would laugh and wave back.

"And that is the story of Crazy Alen."

We sat then and listened, and Mother took a breath because she had been holding it, with one hand over her mouth, and I thought of death. Death never seemed funny to me. All I knew of it was when I had been sick and thought I would die and was afraid, or in the fall when we killed and killed. But it was impossible to think of Crazy Alen without smiling and that meant I was smiling at death, laughing at death and the picture of Alen with his arms and legs out and the foreman trying to get him down the trail.

There were many questions I wanted to ask and I knew Wayne wanted to ask some as well but we didn't. We never did. The stories were just there, not something to be questioned and opened up. Uncle David just told them and they came from him and went into us and became part of us so that his memory became our memory. But nothing about them was ever questioned.

Until he told the story that broke things.

It is strange, the way it happened, strange and kind of inside-out. It all came down to how Wayne felt about the stories. I always thought of them as just stories and didn't think they were real. I mean I know there probably aren't a man and woman living in a cottage under the sea— probably. Once Mother said the stories were not for believing so much as to be believed in.

But it was different for Wayne. I didn't know

it, but it was different. Somehow the stories had mixed in his mind so they had become a real part of his thinking, so that he believed them. And even when he knew they couldn't be— knew there couldn't be a man and woman living in a cottage under the sea—even then he wanted them to be real, wanted her hair to take the ships down, and by wanting them to be real somehow they became real in his mind. And that's how the trouble started.

There is nothing I could have done about it anyway but if I could have stopped it, stopped the hurt I saw in Uncle David's eyes, I would have given anything.

We had spent a long day splitting and carrying stove wood in because the wind had come around to the northwest and it was picking up into a storm. Father said it would blow for three or four days and drop to forty below when it stopped snowing and blowing and we wanted to be ready for it. Father split with the big double-bladed ax he kept in the ax bin in the granary, each ax so sharp you could shave the hair on your arms with it, just as Uncle David said. Wayne and I weren't allowed to use them, not even to split kindling. They were axes that used to belong to Uncle David and to Nels when they cut wood in the old days and they were something to see. All shining and silver, the two blades on each honed with a small, circular stone. I had seen Uncle David and Nels sharpening them with the stones, sitting with peaceful smiles on their faces while the stone went round and round and I thought it was the same look Mother had sometimes when she was knitting. But I had never seen Uncle David or Nels use the axes and I figured it was because they were so old now that they couldn't use them because it would hurt them somehow.

So Father split wood and I asked to help carry it and Father said yes. I felt like I must have brought in most of a cord by myself, stacking it under the overhang on the porch. When we were done, finally, I couldn't see over the pile. It covered the whole porch and I thought there was enough for two weeks before Father finally put the ax away and we went to milk and do evening chores.

That night it was my turn to crank the separator and change the buckets, and by the time we at last went to the house for supper it was so dark the lantern light from the kitchen window made all the snow in the yard seem to glow. I was so tired my brain felt filled with rags.

Mother had made a big pile of mashed potatoes with meat gravy and I made a little lake of gravy in the middle and ate around the edges until I couldn't eat any more, and then, after Wayne and I did the dishes, we went into the living room.

Father started to carve and showed us how far he'd come along since last time and Mother nodded and smiled and Nels and Uncle David filled their lower lips and talked about how the snow cover was good for the crops next year. Then they talked about work that needed doing, and I was watching the fire through the small window on the stove door and my eyes closed and I was sleeping. Or half sleeping. Just going in and out of it when I heard Uncle David start a story—and it wasn't about Alida.

∿ THE
WOODCUTTER

"It was when I was young but I was old enough to have come to the new country and to the north woods and was working as a cutter.

"In the first winter we cut in the lake country and used the lakes and rivers as ice roads for the teams and sleighs. Boys too young to cut took water sleighs with tanks of water in them and soaked the grooves where the runners ran to keep them slick, and put hay in the downhill grooves to slow the loads so they wouldn't run over the teams. I tell you we moved some wood and those horses got so strong they could haul a load as big as a house down to the rivers where the logs were left on the ice to float down the rivers to the sawmills in the spring floods.

"I don't even know how much wood we cut. One camp didn't speak with another, one company didn't speak with another. We just cut and cut until there wasn't anything left. Where there had been forest so thick you couldn't see ten yards without looking at a giant Norway or white pine, you could stand on level ground and see fifteen miles and nothing higher than a stump when we were done cutting.

"It was sad and most of us wished we hadn't done it when it was finished but it was that way then just as it is now that the forest has started to grow up some again. People just cut without thinking.

"But this isn't a story about the cutting so much as it is about a man who was young then.

"There were many men who were good cutters because that was a time when all men were cutters, and there are stories about most of them. Some could use a saw this way and some could use an ax that way. There were stories of men who could cut a six-inch pine with a single swing of a double-bitted ax and other men who shaved with axes and still others who could make saws and axes sing and weep and bleed. But there was one man who they said could do all these things.

"It was said that no man could use an ax like him. The wood of the handle seemed to grow out of his hands and there was nothing he could not do. Men in the camps would stop work to watch him and this becomes important when you know that men were paid by how much they cut. To stop meant they did not receive pay.

"But he was such a wonder with an ax that they would stop. The young man would walk to a tree and swing and the chips would float off like they were made of air—chopping half the head and more deep with each blow so the tree would almost fly off the stump when he cut through.

"They said many things of him. They said he could put a match in a stump so the head was sticking up and swing the ax with his eyes closed and catch the match perfectly so that it would split and both sides would light.

"And it was true.

"They said he shaved each day with an ax and never cut himself and his cheek was as smooth as a baby's.

"And it was true.

"They said he could take a four-foot piece of cordwood and swing two axes, one in each hand, swing them into the two ends and the wood would split clean and the axes would meet in the middle.

"And it was true. . . ."

Here father caught his breath and looked up sharply and said across the stove:

"But that was you. All those things were about you. . . ."

And I felt Wayne stiffen next to me on the rug. I turned to look at him and saw he was staring at Uncle David so hard he seemed to stare a hole through him. Wayne was mad. No, more than mad, tight with it, tight with mad the way he got when Philly Hansen took him down again and again in front of the girls at school.

Hurt mad.

Mad like to burn with it—Wayne was raw mad and I could tell he wanted to say something but he didn't because we never talked during the stories.

Uncle David coughed a little and spit in the can and looked for a long time at Father and then finished the story. It was about how the young man who was the best cutter of all thought that his new life would last forever only it didn't. None of it lasted. The woods were gone and he was old, and it ended that way but I didn't hear much of it because Wayne kept staring at Uncle David. He kept stiff like wood and staring at him and I knew something was wrong but I couldn't understand what it could be.

And when the stories were done that night and we went up to our room and got under the quilts to hide from the cold, even then I didn't learn because Wayne just turned away and didn't say anything. I knew he was awake because his breathing was tight and ragged somehow. I wanted to talk to him about whatever it was but he said nothing. I tried to stay awake but the whole day of wood and work and cranking the separator and listening to the stories and the heat from the stove and the cold from the bedroom and the warmth from the stacked quilts on top came crashing down on me and I fell asleep almost before my eyes closed.

In the morning we went outside for morning chores and Wayne looked a little funny at Uncle David in the barn but he didn't seem so mad anymore and I thought whatever it was had passed.

But I was wrong, so wrong, and I would see a thing so awful I wished I had never seen it. . . .

Wayne and I have a special place in the granary in back of the oats bin. I guess it isn't very much of a place but it's close and cozy and sometimes we sit there and talk about things. It wasn't something we planned so much as it just happened when we were small and as we got older we just would find ourselves there now and again when we wanted to talk. That day Wayne looked at me and walked toward the granary. I knew he wanted to talk so I followed. It was just after chores and barely light so I left the door open because there wasn't a lantern in the granary and it was pitch dark. Even with the light coming in the door it was still pretty gray.

"He's lying," Wayne said, as soon as I came in. He was sitting on an overturned bucket by the door so I went in and squatted in the corner.

"Who's lying?"

"Uncle David. All the time he's been lying with the stories, just telling us lies."

"But they're only stories. They aren't real. They're supposed to be lies. . . ."

"It's that he put himself up as one of the

heroes—a great thing. That makes it all bragging and not just stories. Bragging makes it all a lie on a lie. How could anyone cut a match in half blindfolded? How could anyone make two axes meet in the center of a log? That's just all lies. It's all lies and he's a liar and a braggart.

"Don't you see? Father caught him at it. Uncle David told lies about himself and that makes it all lies, just lies and lies and lies."

I was surprised to see that Wayne was crying, that it hurt him, this thing of Uncle David and the stories. He was crying and he said over and over:

"Liar, liar, liar. . . ."

And that would have been bad enough but I looked up, over Wayne and there was Uncle David and I knew he had heard most of it, maybe all of it, because his eyes were full of pain; they looked like the pig's eyes just after Father cut its throat and it knew it was going to die. All pain and confused, all fall killing pain and confused Uncle David's eyes were, so hurt and ripped that it seemed he would crumble, and I could not shut Wayne up.

"Lies, all lies, and he's a liar, a liar, a liar. . . ."

I tried to make a sign, to show Wayne, but it

was too late. Uncle David turned slowly and seemed to cave in and walked away and then I told Wayne, finally I got it out, and Wayne felt bad but not as bad as I thought he should.

It was over, and Uncle David was broken and done.

That night we ate supper and it was good but tasted like wood in my mouth. I saw Wayne who usually ate like a granary dog just pick and pick at his potatoes.

After supper we went into the living room and Uncle David didn't tell a story.

Not even the story of Alida.

He sat and rubbed his face and Father talked and Mother talked and even Nels talked but there was no story, none of anything like a story. Just talk of chores and summer crops and Mother spoke a little of the neighbors who were having trouble with a sick baby, and I thought it was like fall and something had been killed.

Here, I thought, in this room a thing has died. I nearly cried and wished Wayne would be hurt for what he'd done.

And another night

And another night.

Nothing like a story—just talk and talk until

we went up to bed. I started to hate Wayne then and think he should be punished—and on the fourth or fifth day after he broke Uncle David we were in the hayloft.

Many times we went into the hayloft to fool around. It was fun to swing on the trip rope that carried the hay up into the barn when we stored it. We would swing from the little landing up under the roof near the top of the loft down on the trip rope and land in the soft hay. It was something I never got tired of because the hay would catch you, just let you sink soft and down, and it smelled nice.

But this time I was still mad at Wayne, mad and sick of him so it went bad. I made a swing and landed on his leg and he squealed a bit and before I could stop it I was on top of him beating him and crying and cursing him for what he'd done to Uncle David.

We fought around the loft and down the side of the hay, only of course he's bigger than me so it wasn't much of a fight. Pretty soon he was sitting on top of me and he gave me a clout that made my nose bleed.

I got madder then and went a little crazy but he still held me down and clamped my arms to

my side while I just squirmed and I was trying
to bite him when I looked up and he wasn't
paying any attention.

The way we had fallen we were jammed back
into the corner where the logs were crossed in
together. Because the barn was very old, some
of the logs had warped so there were small gaps
between them. Father said if it had been a house
he would have chinked it and filled the holes,
but it being a barn they just ventilated the hay
nice and kept it dry—like a big crib.

Wayne was looking at something through the
cracks in the corner and when I saw how interested he was I forgot all about fighting.

He let me loose and I pulled up alongside of
him and wiped blood off my lip and nose and
looked out the crack and saw Uncle David.

In the back of the barn was a large pile of
wood cut in four-foot lengths for shipment to
the paper mills. Father and some other men in
the neighborhood cut the wood each fall and
haul it out to the railroad when the roads get
frozen and slick enough for the bobsleds, and it
brings in a little extra money for Christmas.

Uncle David was standing staring at the pile
of wood. His arms hung down at his sides and

he looked small and sad somehow and I hated Wayne again for what he'd done. I thought it would be right for me to go down to him and touch him, maybe on the hand, and lean against his leg the way I did sometimes but before I could move Uncle David turned away from the stack of wood and walked to the granary.

I thought it was over, that time when I could have touched him, but in a few seconds he came out of the granary.

He was carrying two axes. He had one in each hand, two double-bitted axes, big and shiny and sharp as razors and I knew then, I knew what he had planned and I thought no, no. I must have moved because Wayne put a hand on my arm and held a finger to his lips.

"Be still. . . ."

"But he'll hurt himself," I whispered.

Wayne didn't answer. He'd turned away and was looking out through the cracks again and I did too. I couldn't stop.

I couldn't stop though I didn't want to see it, the way I couldn't stop when they killed the pigs and chickens in the fall—I couldn't stop looking through the cracks.

Back at the woodpile Uncle David took a log

down, studied it, pushed it aside and took another one. The logs looked heavy and big, bigger
than him. He seemed so caved in and tiny, and
when he finally got the log in the right place on
the ground he had to stop and catch his breath
and I thought no, no, no I should run for Mother
or Father and have them stop him because he
should not do this and it will hurt him.

But now it was too late and I knew that, too,
knew that it would be terrible to keep him from
at least trying.

He stood to the side of the log facing it and
held the axhandles, one on each side with the
heads of the axes resting on the ground and all
of him was curved down onto the axes so they
looked like hickory crutches. He was a broken
and tired and sad old man, and there wasn't a
thing he could do, I thought, even to lift the axes:
So awful a thing, the way he stood, the axes
standing at his side, his hands on the handles
and little bits of steam coming from his breath
as he looked down at the log and I thought no.

Please no. And no matter what it would do,
no matter if Wayne tried to stop me, I was going
to run down and tell him that he didn't have to
do this, that it didn't matter.

But now he moved his head up and looked at the sky and the sun caught his face and we could see it plain, see his face in the sun. The wrinkles seemed to leave. The skin seemed to smooth as the sun covered his face.

And his hands tightened on the axhandles and the heads of the axes in the snow, the heads trembled a little and it was as if something came from the earth.

Some thing, some power passed from the earth up through the silver axheads and through the hickory handles and it started in his arms. A little movement, then the arms seemed to swell and his shoulders came up and filled and his back straightened and his whole body filled with it until he was standing straight and tall and I heard Wayne's breath come in and stop and mine did the same.

"He's young again," Wayne whispered and it was not just a whisper but more a worshiping thing, like part of a prayer, and he was right.

Uncle David stood before the log and he was young, and as we watched, as we could not turn away and we watched, the axes started to move.

Up.

They came up from the snow. The heavy axheads came up and out to the side, came up like they were floating on light air, up and up until they were over his head, one on each side, the sun catching them and splashing the silver from the heads down on him like a new light, a life light and they hung there for what seemed like hours, days, hung in the air over his head while we held our breath. And just when it seemed that all things had stopped, that nothing would or could ever happen again, just then they started down.

Down.

So slowly at first the silver heads began to swing down and then faster and faster until they were two silver curves of light, two streaks curving down and around Uncle David so fast they were just a blur coming into the ends of the log.

Thunnnnnkkk!

Such a clean sound. The silver curves went into the log clean and even and the log opened and split and the axes met exactly in the middle with a small metal sound.

"Oh . . ." Wayne whispered but he did not know he'd said it.

"Oh."

For a second, a long second, Uncle David stood

there, the axes touching in front of him and I was crying and Wayne was crying.

"We have to go down there," I said. "We have to go down there and tell him we saw it."

But Wayne held my arm and shook his head and said, "No. It was for him. All for him. Don't you see? If we go down there it will ruin it for him."

And of course he was right because Wayne is sometimes right, and I settled back down into the hay and looked out the crack again.

Uncle David stood tall for part of another second, then the power all went out of him. His shoulders and back curved down again and his arms seemed to settle on the axhandles and he became old, old and bent. He carefully laid the axes on the ground and bent for the log. He put the two split halves back up in the stack, turned so nobody would see them. Then he picked up the axes and carried them to the granary and put them away and came out, spit in the snow once and walked to the house, bent and old and tired and down.

We watched him through the crack all that time. Watched him walk until he was gone inside the house, the two of us crying, and that night when chores were done and we'd eaten a big supper we went into the living room and Uncle David told us about Alida. Then he told a tale about a man who lived in the forest who was so ugly he couldn't be seen and he sent messages of love to a girl on the wing feathers of birds and Wayne listened and I listened and I knew we would listen for always.

after words™

GARY PAULSEN'S
The Winter Room

CONTENTS

After Words™ guide by Lisa Ann Sandell

About the Author

Born in 1939, Gary Paulsen has been a master storyteller for more than forty years. Although he was not very interested in his studies as a boy, Mr. Paulsen became a passionate and devoted reader when a librarian gave him a book to read and his own library card. He would pass hours by himself in the basement of his apartment building, devouring book after book.

When he was fourteen, Mr. Paulsen ran away from home and began to travel with a carnival. This was his first taste of adventure, and he has continued to seek it throughout his life. Spending a summer helping out on a farm; working as an engineer, construction worker, ranch hand, truck driver, and sailor; and racing a few times in the Iditarod, the 1,180-mile Alaskan dog sled race, have provided ample material from which to create his powerful stories.

Mr. Paulsen realized that he would become a writer all of a sudden, while he was working as a satellite technician for an aerospace company in California. One night he simply walked off the job, never to return. He then spent the next year in Hollywood as a magazine proofreader, working on his own writing every night. Soon, he left California and drove to northern Minnesota, where he rented a cabin on a lake. By the end of the winter, he had finished his first novel. He says, "I started to focus on writing the same energies and efforts that I was using with dogs. So we're talking eighteen-, nineteen-, twenty-hour days completely committed to work.

Totally, viciously, obsessively committed to work. . . . I still work that way, completely, all the time. I just work. I don't drink, I don't fool around, I'm just this way. . . . The end result is there's a lot of books out there."

He has written more than 175 books and some 200 articles and short stories for children and adults, and he is considered one of the most important writers for young adults today. Three of his novels—*Hatchet*, *Dogsong*, and *The Winter Room*—are Newbery Honor books, and his works frequently appear on the best books lists of the American Library Association.

Mr. Paulsen and his wife, Ruth Wright Paulsen, an artist who has illustrated several of his books, divide their time between their home in New Mexico, a boat in the Pacific, and adventures in the wilderness.

Q&A with Gary Paulsen

Q: *When did you start writing?*
A: I started writing in my twenties when I walked away from a job and a life because I knew, suddenly, that I had to be a writer.

Q: *What led you to writing fiction for young adults?*
A: I think and have always said that it is artistically fruitless to write for adults. They're already set in their ways, but young people are so much more open to new ideas, new experiences.

Q: *Did anyone help you find your way as a writer?*
A: There were a couple of men who worked at a magazine where I got my first writing job who helped me develop discipline in writing. Other than that, though, it's been trial and error, reading as much as I could, and writing every day that have helped me most as a writer.

Q: *What's your favorite book?*
A: The next one I'm writing.

Q: *Who was your greatest inspiration?*
A: I don't know that I'm inspired by anyone in particular. I love to write, that's all the inspiration I think I have. I can't NOT write.

Q: *As we're getting ready to publish this After Words edition, you're training dogs to race in the Iditarod. How did you start dog racing? How did you come to have such a taste for adventure?*

A: I'd been given a few old dogs and a busted sled when I was dead broke, living in Minnesota, and trapping to make a few extra bucks. I fell in love with the beauty of running dogs, not racing them; that just seemed to be a natural progression. I don't know that I have a taste for adventure so much as I am curious, and I always need to be doing something physically and learning something new intellectually. Perhaps the two together seem adventurous, but that's not my exact intention.

Q: *With so many varied hobbies and interests, how do you find the time to write?*

A: I write every day. The discipline to write each and every day no matter what was drilled into me years ago by some magazine editors, and it's a habit I've never abandoned.

Q: *What is your writing process?*

A: I write whenever, wherever, however I can. I'm not wedded to any one time or style or format. I can write longhand on a notepad or type on my computer or compose in my head. It's not the how that's important, but that it's a daily commitment.

Q: *Where did the idea for* The Winter Room *come from?*
A: Stories I'd heard growing up as a kid.

Q: *How personal is this story? Did you grow up on a farm?*
A: I spent a lot of time on farms when I was growing up, and everyone had tales like this. All the families I ever visited would sit and talk about relatives and friends in the evenings after work.

Q: *You write about the relationship between Eldon and Wayne so poetically and convincingly. Do you have any brothers or sisters?*
A: I have one younger sister, but she's so much younger that I was already grown and out of the house by the time she was born. So I think of myself as an only child because I grew up alone.

Q: *The scene in which Wayne tries to jump onto Charger's back has us in stitches every time we read it. Did you ever try jumping out a barn window onto a horse's back—or any other stunts?*
A: I think every boy who ever spent time on a farm and saw old movies tried that stunt at least once. I've written in other books (*Harris and Me, How Angel Peterson Got His Name*) about some of the other things we tried as kids.

Q: *What is your favorite season, and why?*
A: Winter. Because I can run dogs.

Q: *Is there something specific to farm life that moved you to write this story?*

A: Farm life is very much attuned to smells and sights; it's an extremely hands-on experience, to work on a farm. I just paid attention to the world around me when I was a kid and tried to remember what it had been like as an adult. I think farms and farming are beautiful things and I loved the time I spent there as a child.

America and the Natural World

Unlike many other books, *The Winter Room* begins not with a prologue or an introduction but with a short chapter titled "Tuning." Less than three pages long, it ends with a direct call to the readers: "If books could have more, give more, be more, show more, they would still need readers, who bring to them sound and smell and light and all the rest that can't be in books. The book needs you."

The first step toward better understanding the beautiful world Gary Paulsen has created in *The Winter Room* is to imagine America as a different country—a younger country. Eldon, the narrator, and his family light their house with lanterns, churn their butter by hand, and plow their fields with a team of horses. They have no machines, and live in a farm so vast and remote that a visit to the small nearby town is a special occasion.

For most of the nation's history, that's how the majority of Americans lived. According to the 1790 census, more than 95 percent of the population lived in the countryside, with the remaining 5 percent living mostly in small villages. At the time, the United States had only three large cities, Boston, New York, and Philadelphia.

A hundred years later, however, in 1890, the Industrial Revolution had created a growing demand for factory workers and attracted many to the large cities. Still, only 35 percent of Americans lived in urban areas, concentrated mainly in the North. The rest continued to live a country life, and the majority of the nation's economy relied on agriculture. It was only by 1920—144 years after the Declaration of Independence—that the majority of Americans had moved to large cities, and the life described in *The Winter Room* became increasingly rare.

This move from country to city meant much more than simply changing one's address or living in an apartment instead of on a farm. It meant the loss of a host of traditions and experiences that had defined American life for centuries, most important among which is nurturing the affinity for nature.

The love of nature was a major theme for many celebrated American authors of the nineteenth century. The famous essayist Ralph Waldo Emerson, for example, wrote, "In the wilderness, I find something more dear . . . than in streets or villages." The poet Walt Whitman described the earth as a perfect creature that spoke not as ordinary human beings do but in another, heavenly language: "Syllables are not the earth's words, / Beauty, reality, manhood, time, life—the realities / of such as these are the earth's words."

This bond with nature is evident in *The Winter Room*. The book itself takes its structure from the very turning of the seasons, beginning in spring and ending in winter, with each chapter describing the chores that the narrator and his family must complete before the weather changes.

Yet the nature portrayed in *The Winter Room* is not the ideal nature that Emerson and Whitman wrote about. Instead, it is a much more objective nature, one that is capable of great beauty as well as of great harshness, one that celebrates life but also includes death, and one which people must learn to master if they want to survive. The tasks that the narrator and his brother, Wayne, face every day are tough and demanding: thrashing, stacking, churning, plowing, and chopping. The boys must constantly work to keep the farm running.

Indeed, rural life in America has never been easy, as Mother Nature is capable of many extremes, and even today, with most farming equipment being machine-operated, farmers are still at the mercy of her whims. However, nature also affects those who live in America's cities. When earthquakes, windstorms, and severe rains bring about flooding or destruction in our nation's urban areas, city dwellers may also be reminded of the strength of nature's grasp and nature's ability to influence and affect our daily lives.

Norse Mythology

Many of Uncle David's stories have to do with what he calls "the old country," or Norway. Between 1825 and 1925, no fewer than 800,000 Norwegians—about one-third of Norway's population—immigrated to North America, with the majority settling in the United States, particularly in Minnesota, where Eldon and his family live.

Despite moving to America, it is clear that David and his brother, Nels, like many other immigrants, remain rooted in the customs and stories of their native country, and the stories they tell, recounted in the last pages of the book, borrow heavily from Norse mythology. One of the world's most ancient mythologies, it features a variety of mysterious creatures who fight, die, and are reborn, interacting with people and with nature around them.

The story of Orud the Terrible, for example, recalls several Norse legends. In one, a monster called Selma, whose body is made up of the souls of men who were lost at sea, haunts Lake Seljordsvatn. In another, a giant squid called Kraken, which is the size, legend has it, of a small island, preys on ships and terrorizes sailors. Similarly, Orud's fierce wife, Melena, avenges her kidnapping and death by spreading her hair in long strands and capturing boats as they set out to sea.

Other elements in Norse mythology are similarly designed to explain the natural world's mysteries and paint a picture of the earth that ties together the known and the unknown: Caves are guarded by trolls, streams protected by elves, and the many worlds that make up the universe—the world of man, the world of fire, the world of ice, the world of the dead—are all connected to one another by a giant tree.

Taken all together, these legends serve to explain to people the mysterious things they cannot understand—storms, for example, or death—and reassure them that life continues and flourishes even beyond what they can see and grasp with their eyes and their minds.

Comic Books and Captain Marvel

Eldon and Wayne love to read comics in *The Winter Room*. One of their favorite characters is Captain Marvel, who was one of the early superheroes of comic book fiction. He was created in 1939 by the writer Bill Parker and artist C. C. Beck, and the first Captain Marvel comics were published by Fawcett Comics and then by DC Comics. What distinguishes Captain Marvel from his better-known predecessor, Superman, is that Captain Marvel's alter ego is a twelve-year-old boy named Billy Batson. The story begins when one day Billy, a newsboy, is taken to the lair of the wizard named Shazam. When Billy repeats the wizard's name, he is struck by a bolt of lightning and transformed into Captain Marvel, a grown-up superhero with powers similar to Superman's. It's easy to see why so many kids would have such an affinity for Captain Marvel, imagining that they, like Billy Batson, could become superheroes themselves.

From the 1930s through the 1950s, comic books gained such a high level of popularity that this era became known as the golden age of comic books, and comics became widely accepted as a mainstream art form. This is when the comic superhero first surfaced, and characters such as Superman, Batman, Captain America, Wonder Woman, and Captain Marvel were created. Many of these characters continue to be favorites today, and the comic book continues to evolve and find new audiences.

A Sneak Peek at *The Voyage of the* Frog

He pushed the tiller over hard to the left. The *Frog* was still locked in irons, head up into the wind, but she was nonetheless moving a tiny bit to the rear, and with the helm over hard to one side she would slowly back around side-to the wind again and he could get her sailing. Another thing Owen had taught him: how to do all things without the motor.

But as he held the tiller over he reached for the jib sheet to pull the sail tighter to take the wind when the boat came around, and the sheet was caught on the front hatch which he had forgotten to close.

Normally he would just drop down inside the boat and lower the hatch from inside. But one strand of nylon, a tiny strand from the jib sheet, was hooked on the top of the hatch in a screwhead and he would have to go up on the cabin to unhook it.

That one small thing, that tiny thread hooked on a screwhead, saved his life. Later he would wonder about it, about how the thread in the nylon rope came to be hooked that way—it had never happened before—and he would think on twists in his life, how something as small as a thread could save him.

He let the tiller go again and with one hand on the wooden handrail that was bolted to the top of the cabin he clambered forward, impatient to be sailing, heading home, away from this place in the sea where Owen's ashes were floating.

At the forward hatch he quickly unhooked the caught

thread and dropped the hatch cover in place—it had to be fastened tightly from the inside—and stood to move back to the stern. The jib was luffing in great slaps and it hit him in the face so that he put a hand up to protect himself; that hand pushed the sail to the side and he could see forward, over the bow a great distance because he was standing, and that's when he saw it.

Away to the north, close to two or three miles distant, the swells looked strange. The sky was clear and the morning sun was off to his right. He could see well enough, but it still looked strange. It seemed as if the tops of the swells were flattened somehow. Either pushed flat or . . . or something else. What? Cut off? He stood on tiptoe—silly that, as if raising himself an extra inch or two could help, but it was automatic—and squinted. Maybe it was light, sunlight or something cutting the water off funny.

No. They truly looked different. Not flattened so much as cut. As if a giant knife were cutting the tops off the swells and waves. Without his consciously knowing it, the hair on the back of his neck moved up and his shoulders tightened. So strange. He'd never seen such a thing, never even heard of it. Owen had never mentioned anything like it.

The waves were just cut off clean.

What would cut them that way?

Wind.

The answer came with the sound—an almost quiet moan mixed with a sharp tinkling that he realized was the wind pushing water spray ahead of it in a kind of horizontal frothy rain.

It was wind. A wild wind—a wind stronger than anything he'd ever seen or heard of, a wind without warning out of the northwest. For precious seconds he stood, the cut line of swells moving toward him, stood and stared in disbelief. It just couldn't be wind. There were no clouds in the sky, no fronts coming, no signs of weather at all—yet it was there.

Like a fool, he thought, I stand like a fool. It was a wind to take him, to kill the *Frog* and he had wasted time staring. He ran for the mast and released the jib halyard. The truth is that if such a wind hit the *Frog* with her sails up for whatever reason, she would be driven over and down and sunk in seconds.

The sound was louder now—a hissing moan that had an almost evil resonance to it—but he didn't waste time studying it. He clawed the jib down, wadded it in a ball and—with it still hooked to the forestay—he opened the forward hatch and jammed all of the sail he could into the opening. He pushed the hatch back down. It would not latch, but it would have to do.

No time now. Just seconds. He could smell the spray, salt moistness, being driven ahead of the storm—it must be a storm. Some freak storm. He jumped back to the mast and untied the mainsail halyard. Normally the sail would drop of its own weight, but now the wind was getting stronger—he sensed-heard the scream of it, his hair was plastered and blown over his face—and the main stayed up, held now by the pressure of the wind.

He swore, grabbed at the sail and started to rip it down. Everything was noise—the wailing of a thousand screaming throats in the wind, the slapping of the sail sounding like a cannon. He felt one of his fingernails give on a seam. He kept tearing the sail down.

The top of the hatch! He had to get the cabin top hatch open. He moved along the boom, still pulling at the main, fighting to hold himself upright in the wind, and kicked the sliding cabin top forward. The kick made him stumble, and the wind picked him up almost bodily and threw him out, away from the boat, but he tangled in the safety lifeline, caught himself and pulled back up to the cabin top.

The mainsail was slashing back and forth like a demon gone mad. He couldn't control it. Frantically he attacked, pushing part of it down into the cabin through the open top hatch only to have the wind sweep it out while he was gathering more of the billowing insanity to push down again.

It was too late. There was a momentary—part of a second—hitch in the roar of the wind, a tiny hesitation and the full force of the storm hit the *Frog* like a giant sledgehammer. David had a fraction of time to disbelieve the wind—so strong it sucked his eyelids away from his eyes and pushed the *Frog* sideways, scudding like a leaf—then he tried to lean forward for the hatch opening just as the spruce boom, fifty pounds of laminated wood and metal rail still attached to the mainsail, caught a corner of the storm and slammed across the boat like a sweeping saber.

It caught him full on in the center of the top of his head with a crack that sounded like the boom had broken.

There was an immense, staggering flash of white-red color somewhere in the middle of him—with an exploding pain that covered the whole top of his brain like a burning glove—and he knew, as he fell down and forward into the top of the open cabin hatch, he knew it was too late.

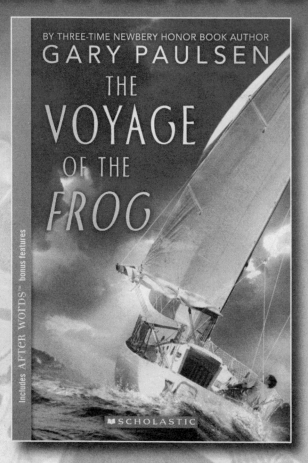